THIS BOOK BELONGS TO:

· · · · · · · · · · · · · ·

For Ian Lawless

First published in Great Britain in 2001 by Andersen Press Ltd., 20 Vauxhall Bridge Road, London SW1V 2SA.
Published in Australia by Random House Australia Pty., 20 Alfred Street, Milsons Point, Sydney, NSW 2061.
All rights reserved. Colour separated in Switzerland by Photolitho AG, Zürich.
Printed and bound in Italy by Grafiche AZ, Verona.

10   9   8   7   6   5   4   3   2   1

British Library Cataloguing in Publication Data available.

ISBN 1 84270 372 2

This book has been printed on acid-free paper

MR BENN
GLADIATOR

David McKee

ANDERSEN PRESS
LONDON

Festive Road was being repaired. At number 52, Mr Benn looked out of his window.

"What a noise," he said. "I think I'll visit the costume shop."

The costume shop was a very special shop that adventures could start from.

A little while later Mr Benn was looking around inside
the shop. He started to chuckle.

Suddenly, as if by magic, the shopkeeper appeared.

"Hello, Sir," he said. "Which one amuses you?"

"The Roman one," said Mr Benn. "Romans made good roads."

"Ah, the Roman gladiator," said the shopkeeper.
"Try it, Sir. You know the way."

In the changing room, Mr Benn put on the Roman clothes
and admired himself in the mirrors. Then he went through the
second door, not the door back to the shop but the door that went . . .
"Where to this time?" he wondered.

He found himself among a group of busy people
in the countryside.
"Mr Benn," said a voice. "What are you doing here?"

The speaker was a large man whom Mr Benn knew from other adventures. "Smasher Lagru," he said. "Fancy meeting you. What are you building?"

"A road," said Smasher. "It will go straight to the city and the Arena."

Just then there was a fanfare of trumpets.

"The Emperor," said Smasher. "We put on a little show for him."

He blew a whistle.

All work stopped. Then one man held up his thumb and another sighted an instrument at it. "Lining up the road," Smasher winked. "It pleases the Emperor and we get a break."

As the Emperor left he called, "Gladiator, bring the big fellow
to the Arena. He'll amuse us."
"What does he mean?" asked Mr Benn.

"He gets men to fight the gladiators," said Smasher.
"I'd forgotten that gladiators fight," said Mr Benn. "Fighting is silly."
"And so say all of us," said Smasher.

At the Arena, Mr Benn joined some worried gladiators.

"Hello," he said. "If you're so worried about fighting, why fight?"

"The Emperor, of course," said a man. "We do as he says or it's thumbs down."

"Thumbs down?" Mr Benn looked puzzled.

"Look," said the man. "If the Emperor turns his thumb down it means a squidging for someone. Thumbs up, they go free. Then there are the lions."

"Lions? Squidging? How awful," said Mr Benn. "I've an idea."
He explained the idea then went to see the prisoners.
"You're right, Smasher," said Mr Benn. "Nobody wants to fight."
Again he explained his plan and said, "I must hurry back to the road."

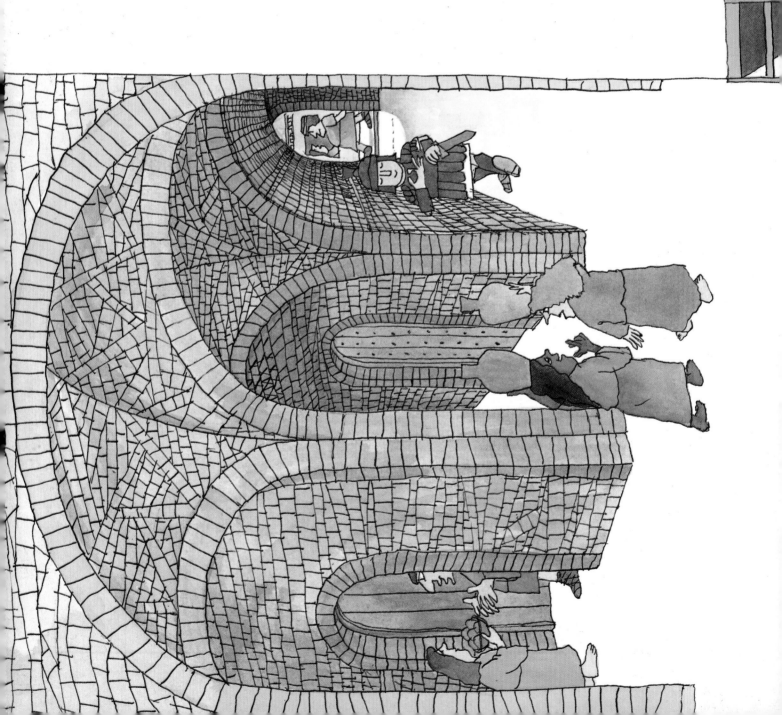

Mr Benn went to the road and returned with the man
with the sighting instrument. "You'll be on top of the Arena wall,
opposite the Emperor," said Mr Benn. "You know what you have to do.
I'm off to see the Emperor."

He found the Emperor about to go to his seat.

"The road is in your honour," said Mr Benn.
"But to lead it straight to you, we need the help of
you and your thumb."

The Emperor smiled smugly. "I've seen the road
being lined up," he said. "I know what to do."

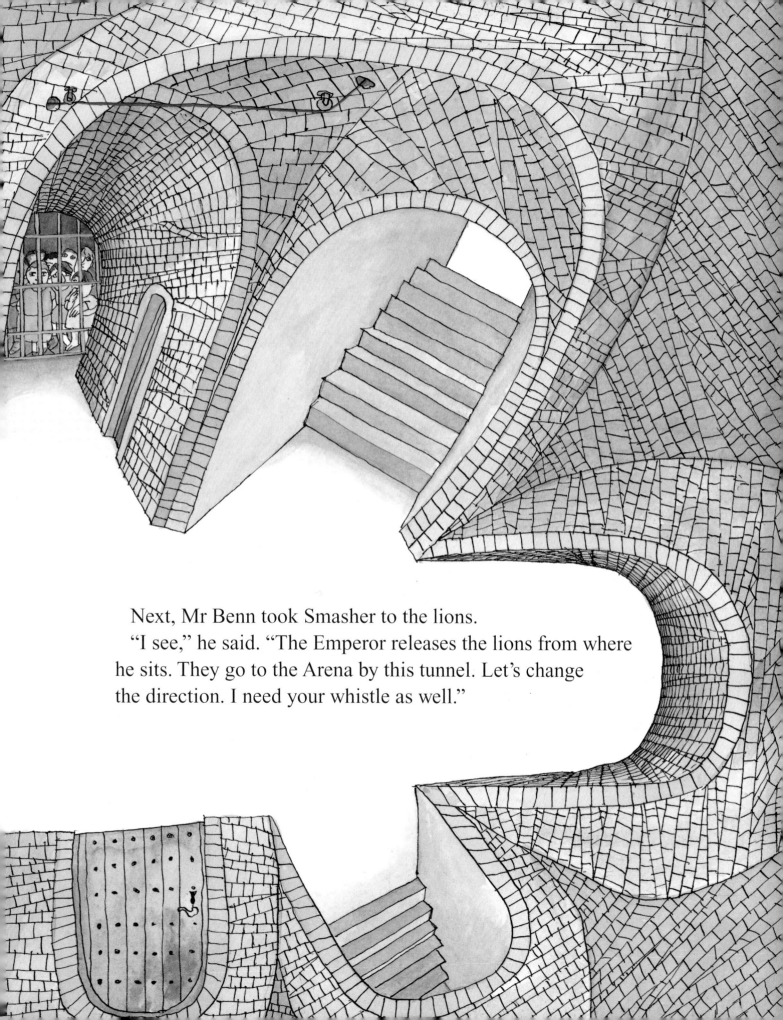

Next, Mr Benn took Smasher to the lions.

"I see," he said. "The Emperor releases the lions from where he sits. They go to the Arena by this tunnel. Let's change the direction. I need your whistle as well."

It was time to enter the arena. Would the plan work?
Instead of fighting the two sides began a kind of
football match. They chased each other and played all kinds
of tricks. Sometimes they even kicked the ball.

The crowd loved it. Only the Emperor was unhappy.
He wanted a squidging.

When at last a prisoner fell, the Emperor prepared for a thumbs down. Mr Benn blew the whistle. Everyone froze. The Emperor stiffened, smiled and held his thumb up. The prisoner left the Arena, free.

After that, whenever anyone fell Mr Benn blew his whistle
and the Emperor held up his thumb for freedom.

The Emperor was furious. "The lions," he roared.

That was a signal. Everyone fell to the ground. Mr Benn whistled, and up went the Emperor's thumb. The prisoners and gladiators cheered and left.

The lions arrived, but not where expected. Thanks to Mr Benn
and Smasher they appeared beside the Emperor. That was when the crowd
decided to go home.

"I liked the way you made him put his thumb up,"
said Smasher.

"He lined up the road when I whistled," Mr Benn winked.

Smasher laughed. "It's time I got back to that road.
See you, Mr Benn."

"I hope so, Smasher," said Mr Benn. "Good luck."

A familiar voice called to Mr Benn: "This way, Sir."

Mr Benn went through a door and into the changing room.
Back in the shop he returned the Roman outfit.

"Keep the whistle as a souvenir, Sir," said the shopkeeper.

As he left Mr Benn turned and waved. "Thank you, again," he said.
"See you soon."

Other books by David McKee

Elmer

The Conquerors

Not Now, Bernard

Three Monsters

Who is Mrs Green?

Zebra's Hiccups

*To find out more about Mr Benn himself visit
his very own website at
www.mrbenn.co.uk*